Little, Brown and Company

Hachette Book Group
1290 Avenue of the Americas, New York, NY 10104
Visit our website at www.lb-kids.com

Little, Brown and Company is a division of Hachette Book Group, Inc.
The Little, Brown name and logo are trademarks of Hachette Book Group, Inc.

The publisher is not responsible for websites (or their content)
that are not owned by the publisher.

First Edition: September 2013

Library of Congress Control Number: 2013933182

ISBN 978-0-316-22833-6

10 9 8 7 6 5 4

CW

Printed in the United States of America

LICENSED BY:

TRANSFORMERS® RESCUE BOTS

The Mystery of the Pirate Bell

Adapted by Maya Mackowiak Elson
Based on the episode "The Lost Bell"
written by Greg Johnson

L **B**

LITTLE, BROWN AND COMPANY
New York Boston

One dreary morning, Cody is reading about an important event in Griffin Rock history. "'Pirates sailed in on a ship called the *Oaken Crow*, and looted!'" he reads. "'Before they escaped, the swashbucklers set fire to the entire island!'"

Heatwave interrupts, "Humans spend too much time thinking about the past."

"Of all the things they stole, the Settlers' Bell was the most valuable. It had hung in the lighthouse tower since the town's founding," Cody explains.

"But what happened to the pirates?" Blades asks.

"Sorry, guys, but my Lad Pioneer troop has a rehearsal for the Founders' Day ceremony tomorrow! We'll finish later."

Just as Cody is about to leave, his dad, Chief Burns, stops him with disappointing news.

"I'm afraid the rehearsal's on hold," the chief says. "A storm is about to make landfall, and we need to button down the town."

Chief Burns signals to the Rescue Bots to prepare for the bad weather.

Rolling to the rescue, the Bots pick up branches from the street, board up windows, and secure traffic-bots.

While the team is building a sandbag wall, Blades brings up the pirates again.

"So, what did happen to them?" the Copter-Bot asks.

"They sailed into a storm like this one," Cody says. "The *Oaken Crow* disappeared, and nobody ever heard from them again!"

Rain begins to fall hard as the team is securing equipment at the marina. A bolt of lightning knocks over a huge shipping container.

The container crashes down and breaks the pier. Cody and the Rescue Bots are washed out to sea!

The storm is now too strong for any human to follow after them, but Chief Burns knows the Rescue Bots will take care of his son.

Soon, Cody and the Bots find themselves in calmer waters, and they go ashore on a deserted beach.

"We're castaways!" Cody exclaims. "Isn't that cool?"

"You know what would be cooler?" Blades sighs. "If my rotor wasn't bent. Then I could fly for help!"

Exploring the island, Cody and the Bots discover a small clearing with a waterfall and a stream. "This is a good place for shelter," Cody says.

"One shelter, coming up!" Heatwave exclaims.

"I can help!" Cody insists.

"I'm afraid this is a job for heavy machinery," says Boulder.

The Bots gather supplies and start building an unsteady structure of rocks, mud, and logs. As Boulder opens the door, the shelter collapses into a pile.

"It's okay, guys," Cody says when he sees the ruins. "I built my own."

Cody's shelter is small, simple, and just right.

"How did you learn to build that?" Heatwave asks.

"Lad Pioneers," Cody says. "See? It pays to learn about history and how things were done in the past."

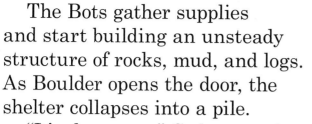

With a shelter built, Cody realizes he's very hungry. The Bots are determined to find their friend some food. They search the beach and tide pool but find very little.

Defeated, the Bots return to Cody without any food. Luckily, Cody has found some food on his own—fish from the stream!

"I'm confused," Blades says. "Did we roll to the rescue or did Cody?"

"Don't worry. You tried," says Cody. "Do you know what I really need? Firewood!"

Once again, the Bots roll into action. They gather lots of wood and use it to make an enormous fire.

"So what's next?" asks Boulder.

"We could tell spooky stories," Cody says. "I know a good one. Five friends are in a dark and creepy forest...."

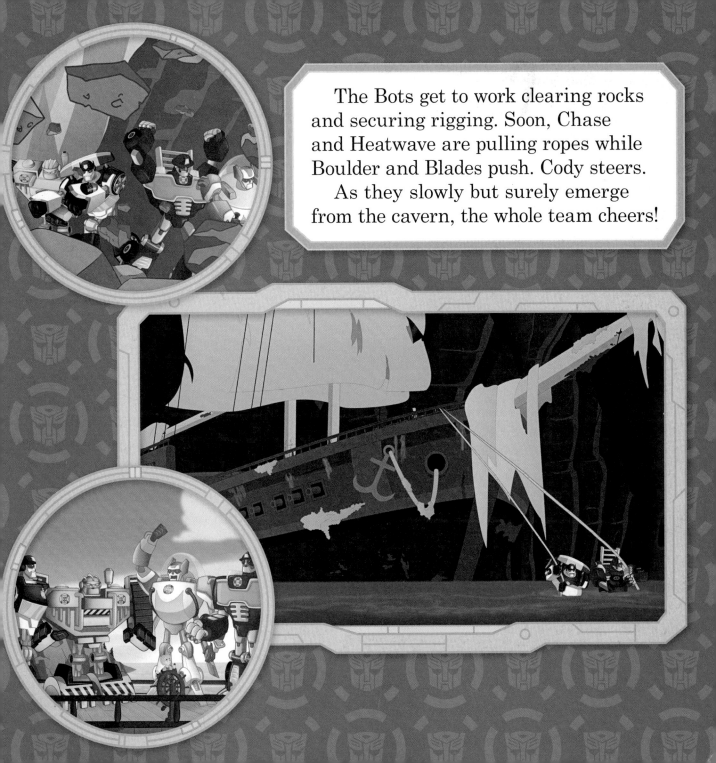

The Bots get to work clearing rocks and securing rigging. Soon, Chase and Heatwave are pulling ropes while Boulder and Blades push. Cody steers.

As they slowly but surely emerge from the cavern, the whole team cheers!

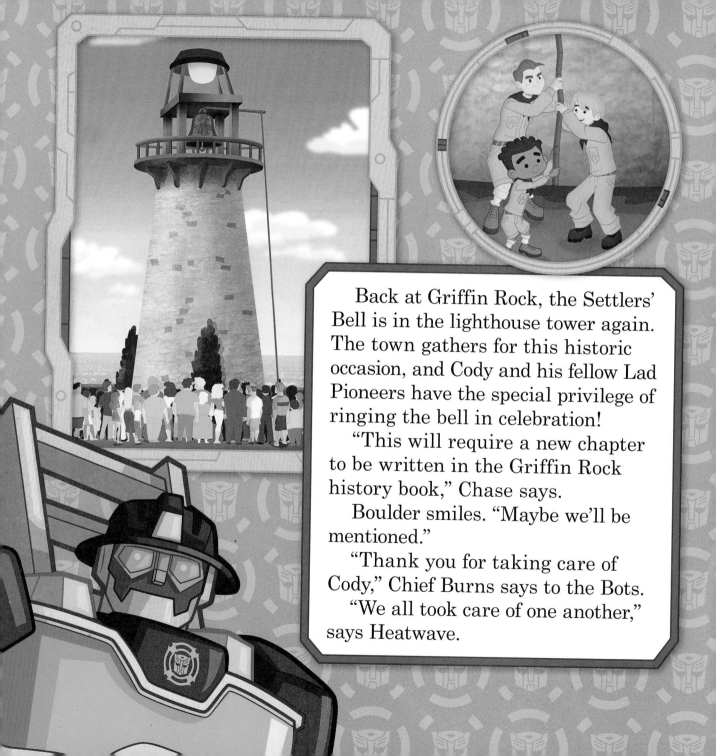

Back at Griffin Rock, the Settlers' Bell is in the lighthouse tower again. The town gathers for this historic occasion, and Cody and his fellow Lad Pioneers have the special privilege of ringing the bell in celebration!

"This will require a new chapter to be written in the Griffin Rock history book," Chase says.

Boulder smiles. "Maybe we'll be mentioned."

"Thank you for taking care of Cody," Chief Burns says to the Bots.

"We all took care of one another," says Heatwave.

This is enough to scare Blades. He jumps up and shouts, "The fire needs more fuel!" as he lifts a large chunk of wood.

"Wait!" Cody exclaims. "Something is carved into that. It's a crow! Like the figurehead on the pirate ship!"

The next morning, Cody and the Rescue Bots go to the ridge where Blades found the crow figurehead.

The group looks for more pirate artifacts. Suddenly, they fall to the bottom of a dimly lit cavern!

"What did we just fall through?" Chase asks.

"A secret hatchway!" Cody announces after some exploring. "And you will never believe what we just found!"

Cody leads the Bots around a bend to reveal the *Oaken Crow* pirate ship floating in a large grotto!

"Astonishing," Chase gasps.

"Looks like it came through there," Boulder says, pointing to an opening blocked by rocks.

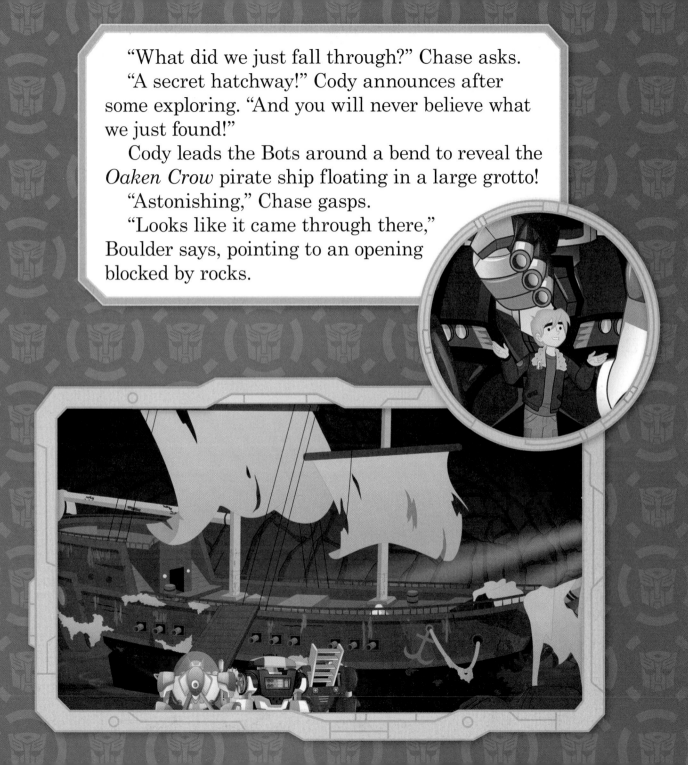

"C'mon! Let's see what's on board!" Cody exclaims.

Cody sprints up the gangplank and leaps on board. The Rescue Bots follow close behind him. There, on the deck of the ship, is the long-lost Settlers' Bell!

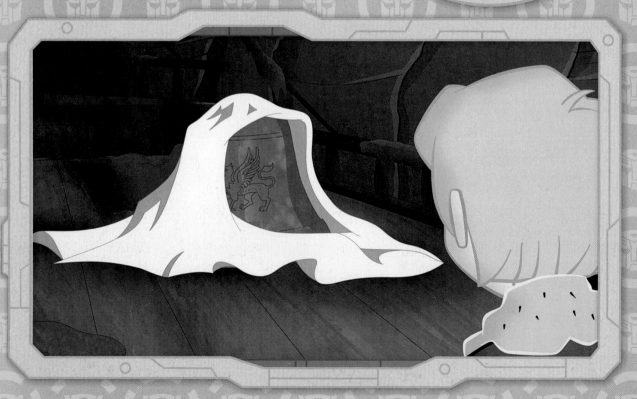

"What a work of art," says Boulder. "I can't believe the Settlers' Bell can finally return home!" Cody says.

Cody quickly realizes that the ship has been stuck down there for centuries. How will they get it out?

"While knowing how things were done in the past is helpful, nothing beats a state-of-the-art Rescue Bot," says Chase.